# Arise,
# Our Rita!

*Hilda Offen*

Happy Cat Books

*For Billy and Dan Smedley*

**HAPPY CAT BOOKS**

Published by Happy Cat Books Ltd.
Bradfield, Essex CO11 2UT, UK

First published 2002
1 3 5 7 9 10 8 6 4 2

A CIP catalogue record for this book is available from the British Library

ISBN 1 903285 28 3

Printed in Hong Kong by Wing King Tong Co. Ltd.

"I am Sir Edward, the Green Knight," said
Eddie.

"And I'm the Lady Juliet," said Julie.

"I'm Sir Edward's squire," said Jim.

"Can I be a squire too?" asked Rita.

"Certainly not!" said Eddie. "You're much
too small!"

"We're off to Foxley Wood with Eric and Tania," said Jim. "We're going on a Dragon Hunt."

"Please let me come!" said Rita.

"No!" said Eddie.

"I *shall* come, so there!" cried Rita.

"That's what you think!" said Julie, and they locked her in her bedroom and ran away.

Rita rattled at the door.
"Trapped!" she thought. "Oh – I know! My
Rescuer outfit!"
She pulled the box from under her bed and
got dressed as quickly as she could. Then she
hurtled through the window.

"I'll soon catch them up," thought Rita and she started to run.

"BOOM!" She went faster than the speed of sound.

"FLASH!" She went faster than the speed of light.

"ZOOM!" She broke the Time Barrier!

Rita travelled back through the centuries until she came to a stop at the edge of a forest.

A man in green was shooting at a target.
"All my friends have run off," he sniffed.
"They say I can't be in their gang because
I'm such a bad shot."
Rita took his bow.
"Watch carefully," she said. "This is how you
do it."

"Thank you, Rescuer," said the man. "I think
I get the idea. My name's Robin, by the way."
"Nice to meet you," said Rita. "Keep
practising."
And she disappeared into the forest.

Before long she met a boy with an axe.
"My brothers say I can't have any dinner till
I've chopped down this tree," he said.

"Give me the axe," said Rita.
"Wham!" She cut down the tree with a
single blow. Out popped a golden goose.
"Ooh - thanks, Rescuer!" said the boy.
"Have an egg."
"How kind!" said Rita. "But I must hurry!"
She could hear someone in the distance
roaring "Fee-fi-fo-fum!"

A giant was bullying a poor farmer.
"Give me your cow!" he roared.
"Quick - hand me your hay-rope," said Rita.

She whizzed round and round at lightning speed. Soon the giant was tied up like a parcel.

"I give in!" he screamed and he hopped away over the fields.
"Would you like this egg?" Rita asked the farmer.
"You could buy a few more cows."

15

Over the next hill a princess was fighting a
Robber Knight. Thud! She tripped over a
stone and fell flat on her face. Rita grabbed
her sword as it flew through the air.

The Robber Knight didn't stand a chance.
Rita made rings round him with her nimble
footwork. He was soon defeated.
"Apologize!" said Rita.
"Sorry!" whimpered the Robber Knight and
he jumped on his horse and galloped away.

"I'm on my way to rescue my brother," said the princess. "A dragon's flown off to the mountain with him."

As she spoke they heard a crackling sound. "The dragon's set the trees alight!" cried the princess. "There's a ring of fire round the mountain – we can't get through."

"Oh yes, we can!" said Rita and she
grabbed the princess and carried her over
the flames.
Higher and higher they flew, up the icy
mountain, until they came to the dragon's
lair.
"Yum! Yum!" they heard him growl. "Roast
dinner tonight."

Rita hid the princess behind a rock and flew
on until she came to a frozen lake.
"Just what I need!" she said and she heaved
the huge sheet of ice from its surface and
flew back the way she had come.

The dragon looked up in
surprise. His hot breath
melted the ice and it
poured down in a torrent
of water. Fizzle! Sss! Out
went the flames. Clouds of
steam rose in the air.

Then Rita gave a mighty roar. The sound
echoed round the mountains and the dragon
fell back in terror.
"Be off with you!" roared Rita.

"Don't worry - I'm going!" said the dragon
and he turned tail and flew away as fast as
his wings would carry him.

Rita carried the prince and
princess back to their palace.
"Thank you! Thank you,
Rescuer!" they cried.
"Time to go, I'm afraid!"
said Rita. "I'm off to the
Future."

ZOOM

FLASH!

BOOM!

BOOM! FLASH! ZOOM! She was back in
Foxley Wood - and there were Eddie, Julie,
Jim, Eric and Tania, all tied to an oak tree.
They had been captured by Basher Briggs
and his gang.

"On guard, Basher!" cried Rita, seizing Eddie's sword. Basher was no match for Rita's skills. She drove him backwards until he tripped and fell headfirst into a stream.

"Run for it!" screamed Basher's gang and they raced off amongst the trees. Basher crawled up the bank and squelched off after them.

Rita untied the rope.

"Oh, thank you, Rescuer!" cried Julie. "How can we ever repay you?"

"Hm!" said Rita. "Well, I've heard you've been unkind to your little sister. Perhaps you could be nice to her for a change."

Eddie, Julie and Jim hung their heads.

"Anything you say, Rescuer," they muttered. But Rita was already disappearing over the tree-tops.

Rita was back in her bedroom when she
heard a key turn in the door.
"Sorry we locked you in, Rita!" said Julie.
"We've come to ask you to play with us,"
said Jim. "You can be a knight."
Eddie tapped Rita on the shoulder with his
sword.
"Arise, our Rita!" he said.